Old Hollow

AMBROSE STOLLIKER

Old Hollow

© 2018 Ambrose Stolliker

www.ambrosestolliker.wordpress.com

www.aurelialeo.com

Stolliker, Ambrose
Old Hollow / by Ambrose Stolliker 1st ed.

ISBN-13: 978-1-946024-20-6
Library of Congress Control Number: 2017958672

Map by Tiphaine Leard
Editing by Luann Reed-Siegel
Cover design by The Cover Collection
Book design by Inkstain Design Studio

Printed in the United States of America
First Edition:
10 9 8 7 6 5 4 3 2 1

To my wife, Tanya, who married an out-of-work writer all those years ago, and stuck by him while he scribbled away at his silly stories late at night.

THE TREE

FORRESTER HOMESTEAD

CHURCH

APOTHECARY

GENERAL STORE

BLACKSMITH

ROAD

ASSEMBLY HALL

OLD HOLLOW

Old Hollow

One

AMBUSH

The Reb horse patrol appeared at dusk without warning, as if conjured out of the driving rain by the Devil himself. Lawson pulled hard on the reins and was nearly thrown from his mount. There were dozens of enemy cavalry pouring out of the failing light, and more on the way judging from the sound of thundering hooves. One of Lawson's men drew a revolver only to be blown from the saddle by both barrels of a Reb shotgun. Horses from both sides collided, sending another one of his men crashing to the ground. He was gunned down before barely raising his mud-stained face out of the muck. In the shadow of a moment, Lawson's small scouting party had been reduced from five to three.

"There's too many of them! Head for the woods!" he screamed.

A bullet whizzed past his ear, and he glanced to his right in time to see one of the Rebels pulling back on his Colt's hammer for a second shot. There was no time to go for his own sidearm. *Lord Almighty, he's got me.* He winced, braced himself for the shot, and prayed the Reb's aim wasn't that good. He didn't hold out much hope, though. From the looks of their short waistcoats and insignia, these were Hampton's boys, and they were among the toughest, finest horse soldiers in either army. Just then, Lawson's horse reared up. The bullet pierced the animal's gut, but somehow it managed to keep its feet when it came back down. One of the men in Lawson's party shot the Reb from his horse before drawing rein and hightailing it into a patch of woods on the opposite side of the turnpike. Lawson's mount whinnied in anguish when he drove his spurs into its flanks, but somehow the animal was able to summon the wherewithal to take off in the same direction as the other scout.

Between the torrents of rain and the darkness of the wood, it was nearly impossible to see, but the captain kept going until the sounds of gunfire became more distant. When he finally did slow down several minutes later, he was heartened to see his sergeant, Jordan "Jordy" Lightfoot, just a few feet behind him. He pulled up on the reins and brought his horse to a stop.

The light in Jordy's dark eyes danced with the same mixture of abject terror and euphoria Lawson had seen in so many men just before and after combat.

"I think we slipped away," Lawson said.

"'Pears so. Don't think those Rebs were lookin' for a scrap anymore n' we were. Rainin' too damn hard. They get you, Captain?"

Lawson shook his head. "My horse. Gut shot. Soon as we catch up with Boyd, I'll see how bad it is."

He didn't need to look at the horse to know the wound was probably fatal. He'd had the same mount since before Antietam and knew every aspect of its gait. The poor animal was laboring and wouldn't last more than an hour, if that. He sighed. The horse had been raised on his father-in-law's breeding farm in Pennsylvania and presented to him as a gift from his wife, Susan, and daughter, Ada. Just one more thing this damnable war would take from him before its end.

He returned his attention to Jordy. "What about you? They get you?"

"Naw. One o' them Rebs took a swing at me with his sticker, but all he got was my sleeve." He showed Lawson where the Reb's saber had slashed through his uniform right above the elbow.

"Well, I guess we got off easy then," Lawson said. "Can't say the same for Crowly or Develin."

"That's for damn sure. Felt bad leavin' 'em back there."

"We didn't have any choice in the matter."

"Hope the Rebs'll give 'em a Christian burial."

"Me, too."

They said nothing more and headed deeper into the woods. They had gone no more than a quarter of a mile before catching up with the other scout, a boy named Emil Boyd. He was slumped over in the saddle with his hand pressed against the right side of his abdomen. When he saw Lawson and Lightfoot approach, he spat blood onto the forest floor and shook his head in disgust.

"Caught one just as I was leaving the turnpike. Goddam Rebs."

Lawson dismounted and handed the reins to Jordy. "Keep an eye out, just in case they decide to give chase." His concern immediately shifted to the young scout. "Let me have a look, Corporal."

He helped Boyd down out of the saddle and eased him against the stump of a massive oak tree. The entry wound was just below his belt. A quick examination revealed no exit wound. *Damn it. Damn it to Hell.* The bullet was still in there.

He looked Boyd in the eye. "I'm not going to lie to you. It's bad."

"Stomach wounds usually are, Captain," Boyd said matter-of-factly, as if the injury was nothing to be concerned about.

He had to admire the boy's pluck, even if it was hidden behind false bravado. All of twenty, if that, Boyd had already been a part of some of the biggest campaigns in Virginia. The glee in his eyes a few months ago when they'd burned the Shenandoah Valley—the so-called breadbasket of the South—had been unmistakable. Boyd hailed from Maryland and hated the Confederacy for the divided loyalties it had sown between so many men in that border state. He had another reason to hate the Rebs, too—he'd been in his first year at West Point when they'd fired on Sumter, forcing him into the Army of the Potomac as an enlisted man instead of with the officer's commission that would've awaited him had he been given the chance to graduate. All in all, there probably wasn't a man in all of the Second Cavalry who bore the South more ill will than Emil Boyd.

He helped the wounded boy back up on his horse, then returned his attention to his own mount.

"I took a gander, Captain," Jordy said. "You were right. Best to put this animal out of its misery now."

Lawson considered. The horse was clearly in anguish. The humane thing to do would be to put a bullet in its head and move on. On the other hand, there was always a chance the Rebs would come back, and if they did, he'd have a better chance of escape if he had a horse under him, even one with a bullet lodged in its belly. If they were forced to double up on Jordy's horse, the odds were good the animal wouldn't be quick enough to get away and he'd lose yet another man under his command. He couldn't take that chance.

He took the reins in hand and pulled the horse's head up so he could look it in the eyes. "I'm sorry, old boy." The horse nickered. "Just get me a little farther. Can you do that? Just a little farther?" The horse snorted. Lawson patted the white patch on the huge animal's forehead. "Good boy," he whispered. "Good boy." He mounted up, trying to ignore the horse's sonorous groans, and said, "Let's get out of this damnable rain.

Corporal, can you keep going?"

"Damn right I can, Captain."

Lawson nodded. "All right." He pointed into the darkness. "I thought I saw a game trail leading up to a plateau of some sort not too far from here. Let's get up a little higher and see what we can see."

They headed deeper into the woods. Rain ran down the brims of their hats and into their eyes, making it almost impossible to see more than a few feet in front of them, but eventually, they came upon the game trail Lawson had spotted. It led up for two miles to a bluff that overlooked the valley. Far below to the south, they could see the fires of a large encampment.

Jordy shook his head. "I reckon that's Hampton's bunch. Old Marse Bob can't be far away."

Lawson cursed under his breath. *Three damn days we've been looking for Lee.* His eyes fell on the turnpike below where, even at this distance, he could see the shadowy movements of Hampton's Cavalry on the move. "Turnpike's all jammed up with Reb horsemen. Best to stay off the road."

"How we gonna get back to Sheridan then, Captain?" Jordy said. "We're eyein' Bob Lee's backside. Someone's gotta get this back to the general."

Lawson glanced at Boyd, whose pallor had turned ashen, then shot a hard stare at Jordy. "I'm well aware of the situation, Sergeant. Thank you."

The finality of his tone cut off any further protest from Jordy.

"Captain?" This was Boyd. "The sergeant's right. We got to get this information back to Sheridan's camp. You two leave now, you can make it there by day after tomorrow."

"That's enough, Corporal," Lawson said. "I've already lost two men tonight. I'm not leaving anyone else behind." Then, to Jordy, "Give me the map."

Jordy fished it out of his saddlebag and handed it to his captain.

Before long, Lawson jabbed a finger in the middle of the map. "There. Old Hollow."

"That's got to be at least ten miles from here, Captain."

"Good. Ten miles from the Reb army might just suit our needs."

"If we can get there before..." Jordy said in a low voice, throwing a sideways glance at Boyd at the same time.

Lawson felt the urge to upbraid him right then and there. Doing so, however, would do Boyd no good. Something told him it was critical that, as the commanding officer, he maintain the appearance of calm. "He'll make it," he said firmly.

"Town looks pretty small an' cut off," Jordy said. "You're right, it might just work for us. But what if whoever's there don't take too kindly to Yankees?"

Lawson gestured at the valley below with the rolled-up map. "This is secesh country, Jordy. I don't give a damn how they feel about Yankees. Now, let's move like we've got a purpose."

Jordy nodded. "Old Hollow it is then."

Lawson took Boyd's horse by the reins and led him back down the game trail and into the darkness.

Two

OLD HOLLOW

Two miles down the trail, Lawson's horse gave out. He took out his Colt, a .44 caliber Dragoon pistol, and pressed the barrel to the animal's temple, but when it came time to pull the trigger, he found he couldn't do it. Jordy dismounted and pulled his sidearm. The booming shot seemed to die away quickly, as if swallowed by the night and the pelting rain.

"Best damn horse in the Second Dragoons, Captain. I'm sure sorry."

"He saved my life," Lawson said, the sadness in his voice unmistakable. "He took that Reb bullet for me."

Jordy patted him on the shoulder and mounted back up.

Lawson went over to Boyd. The boy had gone from ashen to almost white in the span of twenty minutes.

"Mind if I hitch a ride with you into town, Corporal?" Lawson asked, trying to inject some cheer into his voice in an attempt to keep up Boyd's spirits.

"Not at all, sir."

Lawson pulled himself up into the saddle behind Boyd and took the reins.

"Sorry about your horse, sir."

"It's just a horse. You, on the other hand, are irreplaceable. Let's move double time now, the trail looks pretty clear up ahead."

They rode through the rain until dawn. Several times along the way, Lawson had to wake Boyd up. He'd seen wounds like his before. The few who'd survived such injuries had invariably been the ones who'd managed not to fall asleep. Still, unless there was a surgeon where they were headed, he didn't give the young corporal much in the way of odds. Part of him started to question whether he'd made the right decision keeping the party together instead of heading back to Sheridan to report what they'd found. As soon as the thought entered his head, he chided himself for being so cold. *What were you supposed to do? Leave this boy behind to die alone in the woods? Maybe you've been at war too long, Benjamin. Maybe it's made you too hard-hearted. What would Susan say if she knew you were thinking this way?*

Up ahead, the woods began to thin out.

Jordy pointed. "That's a road of some kind. Think maybe we're close?"

"I hope so," Lawson said.

They emerged from the woods onto a dirt road surrounded on both sides by giant Virginia live oaks. A small wooden post leaned heavily toward the right-hand side of the road. Affixed to the post was a sign: OLD HOLLOW. There were no other markings to denote population or when the town had been founded.

"This is it." Lawson prodded Boyd. "We're here, Corporal. We made it."

"Tired," the boy whispered. "Cold."

They trotted up the road just as the sun broke through the clouds in the pale gray sky. The dawn light cast a weary, blue glow over what Lawson guessed was the town's main square. It consisted of a mix of wood and brick buildings. There was an assembly hall, a church with a high steeple, a post office, a general store, a hostler, a blacksmith, and even an apothecary.

"Anything 'bout this place seem off to you, Captain?" Jordy asked.

"You mean how it doesn't look like the war's been anywhere near it?"

"Yep."

For the most part, even the remotest towns in Northern Virginia had been touched by the fighting in one way or another over the last five years. This one, however, appeared to be an exception. Though most of their windows were dark, the buildings were in remarkable condition. Maintaining buildings required manpower, something the vast majority of towns in this part of Virginia were lacking with most of the fighting-age men still in the field with Lee's army.

"Doesn't look like either side's been here foragin', sir," Jordy said. "Coulda sworn Sheridan's Corps had hit every town this side of the James. The Rebs, too."

Lawson nodded. "Very peculiar." He scanned the town again, searching for any sign of life until Boyd's groans prompted him to tell Jordy, "Let's push on a bit."

Almost as quickly as it had appeared, the town was behind them. For the first time since the encounter with the Rebs on the turnpike, Lawson started to get nervous. He'd gambled coming all this way and now it looked like there was no one here to try and help his wounded man. His eyes fell back on the buildings they'd just passed. *Best we can probably do is get a fire going and make him comfortable. It's in God's hands now.*

"Captain, you see that?"

Lawson turned. Jordy was pointing at a hilltop a few miles away. Nestled at the top of the hill was a house. The glow of a faint light emanated from one of the house's upper windows.

"Let's go."

Jordy fell in behind Lawson. When they came within a few hundred feet of the house, both men drew their sidearms. The house was two stories and had a wraparound porch with a barn for horses and livestock off to the side. Like the buildings in town, both structures were in good condition, not at all like the run-down homes he'd encountered scouring this part of Virginia in search of Lee's army.

Lawson and Jordy dismounted and hitched their horses to a post not far from the porch.

"Help him down," Lawson said. "I'm going up."

He walked up to the front door, holding his pistol behind his back, and gave it three hard raps.

After a few moments, a young woman opened the door. Lawson pegged her age at fifteen or sixteen. She gave him an expectant look, but didn't say anything.

He cleared his throat. "Good morning. Is your mother or father at home, young lady?"

"Father's dead. Mother's inside."

"I see. Fetch her, if you would."

The girl didn't move, nor did she avert her eyes as he had expected her to do after delivering his order.

He frowned. "I said fetch your mother, miss."

"Yankee soldiers." She almost spat the words out. "Are you going to kill me and my mother now, too?"

"I'm not in the habit of answering the questions of young girls," he said, glowering at her. "Now fetch your mother."

The girl looked him up and down, then turned away. As she went, Lawson got the distinct feeling he had just been appraised and found wanting. Despite the fact that he was tired, cold, hungry, and shepherding a perhaps mortally wounded man deep through enemy territory, he had to stifle a laugh at her boldness. A moment later, a woman came to the door. She appeared middle-aged.

"Yes, sir?"

He remembered himself and removed his hat. "Captain Benjamin Lawson, ma'am. Second Dragoons, United States Cavalry, at your service."

The woman glanced behind her, then took a step out of the house and closed the door. "Mrs. Nan Forrester, Captain." She glanced past them. "And those are your men and horses?"

"They are. Mrs. Forrester—"

She moved closer, and whispered, "Please, sir, you must listen to me and listen well."

"Ma'am?"

"Get back on your horses. Get back on your horses and ride away. Please, take my daughter and I with you, take us away from here, now—"

"I'm afraid I can't do that, Mrs. Forrester. I've got a wounded man who needs a fire, water, and a warm bed if you can spare it for a few hours."

The woman looked past Lawson at Jordy, who had slung Boyd's arm over his shoulder and was now walking him toward the house. She looked back at Lawson.

"Captain," she began, "you and your men cannot stay here. It's too dangerous—"

"We didn't see any Reb soldiers on the way in here. Are they hiding somewhere in town?"

"No. There are no Confederate forces here, sir."

"I don't understand then."

Her eyes moved slightly to the right.

Lawson followed them and saw the girl's face in the window. Her steel gray eyes were fixed on him and his men. He wasn't sure why, but something about the girl made him nervous, the same kind of nervous he felt when he and his scouts were close to the enemy, when a wrong move could mean discovery, which in many cases often led to someone under his command not returning to camp.

The woman whispered, "You would do well to listen to me, Captain. Take me and my daughter with you and ride on."

Still looking at the girl, Lawson replied, "I can't do that, ma'am."

"Captain?" Jordy called from behind. "We goin' in? Boyd's lookin' real bad."

Lawson returned his gaze to the woman. "Please, ma'am. I'm making every attempt to be a gentleman here. I understand there's been hardship on both sides of this conflict, but I have no place else to go at the moment. We mean you and your daughter no harm, I can assure you. I just want a place for my man to rest for a while." *You mean a place for him to die.*

Once again, she looked past Lawson at Boyd. From the look in her eyes, he could tell the woman had all but read his mind.

He leaned in close so neither Jordy nor Boyd could hear. "You've seen my man. We won't be here long."

"Very well," she relented. "But you'll wish you'd heeded me, Captain."
She stood aside.

He nodded at Jordy, who labored past with Boyd. The boy could barely keep his feet now.

"There's a bed in the back room," Nan said. "Tessa, show these men where it is."

The girl named Tessa led Jordy and Lawson into a small room in the back of the house containing what Lawson guessed was the marriage bed. He turned and nodded at Nan, then saw to it that Boyd was laid comfortably down.

"Water?" he said to Tessa.

"There's a well in back." With that, she left the room.

Jordy raised his brows. "That's a girl who could use a lickin' or two, you ask me."

"Get Boyd some water, please," Lawson replied, ignoring the remark. Then, he asked the wounded man, "How do you feel, son?"

"Belly hurts something awful, Captain. Feels like it's on fire."

He nodded. "Jordy's getting you some water."

"I'd prefer whiskey."

"I don't doubt it." Lawson said, smiling. "Rest easy now, Corporal."

He left the room and found Tessa and her mother sitting at the table. "Ma'am? Would you happen to have a store of whiskey somewhere? Corporal Boyd is in great pain."

"Whiskey is the Devil's water, Captain. We don't truck with it."

He sighed and scanned the room. On the wall over the hearth was a framed daguerreotype of a man with a long beard. He was dressed in a Confederate uniform. Resting on the mantle under the photo was a formal dress saber, and a superbly made one from the looks of it. He walked over to the hearth to get a closer look at the sword. A name was inscribed in the silver sheath: Maj. Robert Forrester, First Virginia Cavalry.

"Is that your husband, ma'am?"

"Yes. Robert was killed at Gettysburg."

He turned to her. "I'm very sorry."

She sniffed. "Spare me your empty sympathies, Captain."

Lawson frowned. "Despite what you may think you know about Yankees, most of us didn't want this war. I'll be glad when it's over and I don't have to see men die in places like Gettysburg any longer."

"You were there?"

"Sergeant Lightfoot and I were, yes."

"Yet you somehow survived."

"By the grace of God." He glanced back at the daguerreotype. *Could we have been at the Point together?* "Was your husband a West Point man?"

"The Citadel. Class of '46."

"I see. Fine institution." Silently, he wondered to himself whether he had ever come across Major Forrester over the years. The Second Dragoons had tangled with the First Virginia numerous times, and

Lawson had always come away with the deepest respect for the regiment. Had he and Forrester unknowingly crossed swords? Had the Confederate major taken a shot in anger at him in some skirmish along some nameless patch of road? Had he fired his weapon at Forrester somewhere in Pennsylvania, perhaps sending him to his grave? Sometimes, it was the confusion and anonymous savagery of battle that tormented him the most when he tried to sleep at night. How many men—how many fellow Americans—had he killed in the last five years? He had no way of knowing. Too many, that much was certain.

"Captain. Got the water."

The sound of Jordy's voice brought him back to the present.

"Good. See to him, will you, Sergeant? I'm going into town. Mrs. Forrester, we passed an apothecary earlier. I assume there is a doctor or surgeon nearby?"

Nan touched his arm, surprising him. "Captain, I am begging you, forget the doctor and take us out of her—"

"Mother, don't tell them anything! You know the rules!"

"Quiet, Tessa!" Nan turned back to Lawson. "Sir, you haven't the vaguest notion as to what you've stumbled onto in Old Hollow. If you are the God-fearing Christian I believe you to be, you will listen to me—"

"The hell's she on 'bout, Captain?" Jordy interrupted. "Boyd needs a doctor *now*. You want me to go git 'im?"

He raised a hand that told Jordy to back off. "Mrs. Forrester, I don't have time for histrionics, and neither does Corporal Boyd. Now please, I will ask you one more time, and one more time only, is there a doctor nearby that can see to my man?"

"Captain, if you go into town, you will not come back," she told him.

"Mother!" Tessa hissed. "You'll be punished!"

Lawson jabbed a finger in the younger woman's direction. "That's quite enough, miss. Mrs. Forrester? The doctor. Please."

Mrs. Forrester's head fell. "Dr. Clemens. He opens the apothecary at first light."

"Thank you." Then, to Jordy, he said, "See to Corporal Boyd."

"Maybe you shouldn't go alone, Captain. No tellin' who may be hidin' back there, waitin' to take a shot at you. Wouldn't want to see you hurt with things windin' down the way they are now."

Both Tessa's and Mrs. Forrester's faces registered undisguised distaste at the inference in Jordy's remark. Lawson understood their feelings, though. The South's defeat was inevitable and, by his estimation, surrender would come in the next few months or by high summer at the very latest. It would be a bitter pill for their side to swallow, especially given all they'd lost. His eyes went back to the photo of Major Forrester.

"Mrs. Forrester assured me there are no Rebs in town, and I believe her. I'll be fine."

"But, sir—"

"You said it yourself, Boyd needs a doctor now. If I wait, he'll die."

Jordy stepped close to him. "Sir, you an' I both know he's a dead man."

Lawson nodded. "I know, but I have to try. Even if it means finding someone who can make him more comfortable."

"Yes, sir," he said, his reluctance to let his commander leave obvious.

"I don't know how long I'll be. Try to keep him awake. It's his best chance of survival." As he walked past, he said, "And Sergeant? Be vigilant."

"You as well, Captain."

Lawson nodded and left the house.

Three

SHELTER

When Lawson's mounted form disappeared behind the grove of trees at the bottom of the hill, Jordy turned and went back inside to look in on Boyd. He found the young corporal with his eyes closed, bathed in sweat.

"C'mon, youngster, step lively now," he said, nudging him. "Give yourself a chance to pull through."

He barely had the strength to lift his eyes to Jordy. "You and I both know that isn't going to happen, Sergeant."

"Don't talk like that."

"I'm just sorry I have to die in this Reb's house. I'd've rather bought it on the battlefield. Hell, back on that damn road where Hampton's men jumped us."

Before Jordy could react, he heard Tessa's voice behind him.

"You shouldn't talk that way about someone when you're a guest in their house, mister."

Jordy got up and went to the door. "Someone ought to teach you that listenin' in on others' conversations ain't what most people consider polite."

"And someone ought to teach *you* that insulting your host isn't what we Virginians consider polite, either."

Jordy took her by the arm—not gently—and pushed her into the kitchen. Mrs. Forrester stood when she saw her daughter being manhandled and started to protest.

"Ma'am, save it. You an' your daughter here oughtn't to make the mistake of assumin' I'm a gentleman like the captain. I ain't. He's an officer an' a West Point man. I'm just a dumb dirt farmer from Kentucky an' a mean horse soldier to boot. I suggest you keep your daughter under control, or she's gonna find my foot firmly planted in her ass. Do we understand each other?"

"Yes." Mrs. Forrester said, cowed by his threat.

"Good."

Tessa watched with eyes full of contempt as her mother sat back down like a dog slinking away with its tail between its legs. Then, trading contempt for defiance, she glared at Jordy.

He pointed at her. "Wipe that sass off your face before I slap it off, missy. I ain't gonna warn you again."

Tessa scrunched up her face into a forced smile, then turned her back on the towering cavalryman.

Shaking his head, he went back inside to Boyd and slammed the door.

"Captain better come back before I paint that little girl's back porch red," he said, sighing as he took a chair from the corner of the room and sat down next to Boyd.

"You won't get an argument out of me, Sergeant. Maybe if we'd dispensed a few more beatings before Sumter, these people would have thought twice about secession."

"Maybe," Jordy said, although he doubted it. Though he'd never considered himself the sort of man who understood or cared much for politics, the war had always seemed inevitable to him, even before the first shots had been fired. If asked, he would not have been able to explain why he felt that way, except to say that based on the savagery he'd witnessed over the last five years, both sides had been committed to their present course from the outset and to the bitter end, the consequences be damned.

"You just rest now, Emil," he said. "Captain'll be back soon."

"I'm burnin' up. Hope he lays his hands on some whiskey."

"If anyone can do it, the captain can."

Boyd nodded. "You known him for a long time, Sergeant?"

"The captain? Since Bull Run. Think he got assigned to the Second right outta the Point. Back when they still called us Dragoons." Jordy's expression soured. At the start of the war, the Union army's entire mounted arm had been reorganized and expanded, and the Second Dragoons—a designation the regiment had held since well before the war with Mexico— had been renamed the Second U.S. Cavalry. In official circles, the regiment was referred to by that name and that name only, and to do otherwise would have been a serious breach of military protocol. Amongst themselves and out in the field, however, the men of the Second still called themselves Dragoons, and did so with a great deal of pride.

Jordy continued, "I been with the Second since 'bout '51. Seen lots of commanders come an' go. When the war broke out, we saw some action under Captain Armstrong in Company K when McDowell pushed into Virginia the first time."

"Armstrong? That's the son of a bitch who went over to the Rebs, isn't it?"

"Sure is."

"Glad I missed that fight then. Wouldn't have wanted to serve under a traitor."

"You're right to be glad. Losin' at Bull Run was tough to swallow. Between you an' me, I got tired of gettin' pushed around by Lee an' his boys those first few years. Nice to be on the winnin' side for a change, ain't it?"

"We haven't won yet."

"We will. An' when we do, I'm gonna hightail it outta the army an' head home to my Alvena. I never have to fire another shot in anger again it won't be too soon."

"You, Sergeant? I thought you loved to fight the Rebs."

"No, *you* love to fight the Rebs. I just wanna survive it an' go home. Anyways, what'd you wanna ask me 'bout the captain?"

Before he could answer, Boyd was wracked by a violent cough. When he glanced at the hand he'd used to cover his mouth, he saw large specks of blood on his fingers. He let his head fall back to the pillow. "Guess it won't be too long now."

"You talk like that again, Corporal, an' I'll thrash you. Now what'd you wanna know 'bout Captain Lawson?"

"Just wondering, is all. You think he's going to get in trouble when he gets back to Sheridan? For not trying to get the information about Lee to the army?"

Jordy shrugged. "Who in Hell knows? Sheridan finds out, I reckon he's gonna be none too happy."

"What would you have done?"

"Don't matter. I ain't an officer. I just follow orders."

Boyd looked out the window. It was midmorning now. He sighed. "Well, whatever happens, I hope he makes out all right. He could have just left me back there in that forest."

Jordy patted his arm. "You just rest easy now, son. Let the captain look after himself."

Four

PREACHER JOHN

The sun climbed higher into the morning sky as Lawson galloped down the hill toward the heart of Old Hollow. Upon reaching the outskirts of the town, he saw several lights had appeared in the windows of some of the buildings, and a handful of men and women were out and about taking care of the various chores associated with opening up their shops. It was the men that drew his curiosity, though. Most of them appeared to be healthy and of fighting age. Why weren't they with Bob Lee's ragtag Army of Northern Virginia? Last he'd heard, Jeff Davis was so desperate to replenish the ranks of his armies that any man between the age of seventeen and fifty had been conscripted. There were even rumors that the Confederate Congress was close to mustering in slaves to fight. *By all rights, these men have no earthly reason to be anywhere but with Lee.*

The men and women paused whatever they were doing to watch the strange Union soldier on horseback as he passed. The expression in their eyes was an unmistakable combination of disbelief and hostility. He met their gazes with as neutral a look as he could, trying hard not to let on how afraid he really felt. Upon reaching the apothecary, he dismounted, tied his horse to the hitching post, pulled the carbine from the saddle holster, and turned to face the townspeople. He nodded at them, then walked up to the apothecary door and knocked.

A man who looked to be in his late fifties or early sixties opened the door, gold-rimmed spectacles hanging down the bridge of his nose. When he saw who had knocked, he drew up short, startled.

"Dr. Clemens?"

"Yes?"

"Captain Benjamin Lawson, Second Dragoons, United States Cavalry. I have need of your services up at the Forrester house."

"Services?"

"You're a doctor, yes? A surgeon?"

"I am."

"Good. I've got a wounded man who needs attention. Please, come with me."

Clemens searched the road behind Lawson. Then, his voice full of disbelief, he asked, "Did you come to Old Hollow alone?"

"No. As I said, one of my men was wounded late last night. I brought him here in the hopes of finding a doctor, which, if you are to be believed, I have done. His wound is serious, so I'll ask you again to come with me, sir."

Clemens shook his head. Then, he repeated, "You came here *alone*? No regiment?"

"Doctor, please. Time is of the essence." He tapped the carbine's barrel in his open palm. "We must go."

Clemens's eyes went to the weapon. Then he shook his head and signaled for Lawson to follow him inside. "I'll get my bag."

"I'll wait here. And when you come back out, doctor, do so with your hands where I can see them, understood?"

"Understood. Captain, was it?"

"That's right."

Clemens nodded and went inside. A few minutes later, he reappeared, this time wearing a dark frock coat and carrying a surgeon's bag. He held up his hands so Lawson could see he was not carrying a weapon.

"My horse is out back. May I go get it?"

"I'll go with you."

Lawson unhitched his horse and followed the doctor around back to a medium-sized stable. When he saw a half dozen or so healthy horses, each with its own stall, he did a double take.

Clemens caught the look on his face and asked, "Something

wrong, Captain?"

Lawson frowned. "No. Just surprised is all."

"Surprised? By what?"

"Your horses. I didn't think there were any left in this part of Virginia that the Reb army hadn't procured. Last I heard, Lee's men were desperate for remounts. I've even seen some riding mules."

"I wouldn't know anything about General Lee's army." Clemens shrugged and mounted his horse. "I suppose one could say we're just blessed here in Old Hollow."

Lawson filed it away as yet another of the town's peculiarities, and they started back toward the main road leading through town.

"How'd this place get its name, anyway?" he asked.

"Oh, you'll find out soon enough, I imagine."

There was something smug in the doctor's cryptic reply that bothered him. Anxious to get back to the Forrester house to see after Boyd, he said sharply, "Move along, Dr. Clemens."

They rode toward the edge of Old Hollow. As they approached the end of the road, a group of horsemen appeared from out of the grove of trees below the hilly meadow above. Lawson counted six of them. They were armed with shotguns.

They don't look like Confederate regulars. Partisans, maybe? Anger cut through him. *She lied to me.* Then, *You've no one but yourself to blame, Benjamin. You were a fool to come into an unpacified town alone.*

His eyes moved from right to left in search of a quick escape route. He tightened his grip on the reins and prepared to apply the spurs.

"Don't do it, son," Dr. Clemens said. "They'll cut you down before you even get started."

"Damn it to Hell," Lawson cursed through his teeth.

The men raised and pointed their weapons in Lawson's and Clemens's direction.

"You might want to move aside, Dr. Clemens," the lead horseman said. "Wouldn't want you to get shot."

Clemens steered his mount away from Lawson. The horsemen approached.

"What unit are you men with?" Lawson asked when they came to a stop.

The lead man exchanged a look with the other five, who snickered, then turned his gaze on Lawson. "None you ever heard of, Yank."

"Peter, this is Captain Benjamin Lawson of the Second Dragoons. Union cavalry." Clemens told them.

"Is that right? Union cavalry?" the lead man, Peter, repeated.

"Yes, sir, it is," Lawson replied.

"And what brings you to Old Hollow?"

"I'm not at liberty to say."

Peter pointed at Lawson. "Did you hear that? The Yank's not at liberty to say."

The other men laughed.

"One of the captain's men was wounded," Clemens interjected. "We were just on our way up to the Forrester house to see after him."

Peter shook his head. "The preacher wants to see this one." He nodded at two of the other men. "Take his weapons."

The two men brought their horses up on either side of Lawson.

"Now, Captain, you aren't going to give us a reason to shoot you before you've even had the chance to meet the preacher, are you?" Peter asked.

Lawson sighed and handed his carbine and pistol over to one of the men.

"The saber, too," Peter said.

Lawson handed it over. "That was my father's sword. See that it's well looked after. I'll be wanting it back."

Peter trotted over to him. "Yank, where you're going, getting that sword back is the least of your concerns." He turned to the two men who had disarmed Lawson. "You go on up to Nan's house and bring his men back down here." Then, to Clemens, he said, "Go with them, doctor. Just in case there's trouble and someone besides that wounded Yankee needs looking after."

Clemens nodded and left with the two men.

"The preacher's in the church," Peter said to Lawson. "Come with me." He nodded at the other three men to fall in behind him and his captive.

As they rode toward the church, Lawson asked, "Might I ask why you and your men aren't currently in the field with General Lee's army?"

"The last we heard, there wasn't much left of Marse Bob's army. Besides, we don't have much use around Old Hollow for outside conflicts."

Lawson frowned. *Outside conflicts? We're within a day's ride of **both** armies!*

Peter continued, "On the other hand, we don't have much use around here for Yankees, either."

They arrived at the church a moment later and dismounted. The church's high, double doors were open. Peter took Lawson by the arm and led him up the steps, then inside and down a center aisle that divided two long rows of wooden pews. Sitting alone in the middle of the front most pew was a man dressed in black. The man did not stand when Lawson was presented to him.

"Preacher John, this is Captain Benjamin Lawson. Sheridan's cavalry, if I'm reading his insignia correctly," Peter said. "He's here with two other Yankee soldiers. I sent Hyde, Gorman, and Dr. Clemens to bring them back down here."

The man called Preacher John nodded at Peter, then studied Lawson for several minutes before saying anything. Finally, he asked, "You and your men. You are scouts, yes, Captain?"

"As I told this gentleman a few moments ago, military protocol precludes me from discussing what brought us to this part of Virginia."

"Of course it does. But one could easily deduce that three Union cavalrymen this far from the Yankee army are either lost or looking for something. That something, I would hazard to guess, would most likely be the location of General Lee's army. That would make you scouts. As to what brought you here, that I already know. Your wounded man."

Lawson glanced around the church. It was then that he noticed that there wasn't a single cross to be seen—not at the altar and not at the pulpit. His eyes fell on a giant mural on the back wall of the church, right behind the altar.

The mural depicted a massive, ancient tree with hundreds of thick, angry limbs. The limbs looked startlingly like monstrous, knobby hands. At the center of the tree was a great black hole, from which poured what appeared to be a legion of dark, wispy figures with wings. In an arc over the depiction of the tree was an inscription written in coal black: *Come Forth, O Dark Ones, and Avail Thee of Our Blood.*

Lawson backed away. "What in God's name?"

Preacher John nodded at Peter, who took hold of Lawson's arm again.

"What in God's name indeed," the preacher said, standing up then. "Not the god you're thinking of, though."

The captain turned to him. "Who *are* you people?"

He came toward Lawson, his dark eyes dancing with delight. "That, Captain, is what you are about to find out."

Five

CAPTURED

"**Let me ask you something** else, Sergeant?"

"You ought to rest, Boyd. Save your strength." When he saw the look of defeat in the boy's eyes, he added, "What'd you wanna ask?"

"It's about Captain Lawson, sir."

"Corporal, you're like a company bugler can only play one note with all these questions 'bout the captain."

"Guess I'm just curious is all."

"Curious 'bout what exactly?"

"Like what's a captain in the Second Dragoons doing riding around with a couple of scouts? Most captains in Sheridan's cavalry are company commanders. Some even command battalions."

Jordy considered before answering. "Let's just say some men can't let it go when soldiers die under their command. It eats at 'em, at their insides. I think maybe the captain's a man like that."

"I don't understand."

"Well, the captain *did* command a company. Till Gettysburg. Before you joined the Dragoons. I guess he just saw one too many a man die under his command an' that was it. He warn't ever the same after that. Transferred to the scouts an' took me along with him. Maybe he figured the less men under his command, the smaller the chance he might get any of 'em kilt. Why you think he brought us here instead of ridin' back to Sheridan? That's why you got to try an' hold on, son, till the captain can find a doctor, y'hear?"

"Yes, Sergeant."

"All right, you rest now. No more questions 'bout the captain or anythin' else. Rest now."

Boyd closed his eyes, and this time, Jordy didn't have the heart to tell him to try and stay awake. From the look of him, it wouldn't be long now. A few hours at the most, maybe. He was surprised he'd held on for this long. Shaking his head, he went out to the kitchen area where he found Nan and Tessa arguing.

"I want this, Mother!" the girl said, her voice rising in volume. "It's what I was born for!"

Jordy stamped his foot. "Keep it down, the both of you. Corporal

Boyd is sleepin'."

Nan stood and went up to Jordy. "Please, Sergeant. If your captain won't listen, you have to. You are in great danger here, *great* danger—"

"I heard you tell Captain Lawson there warn't no Rebs here. You lyin' 'bout that?"

"No. But the Rebels aren't what you should be worried about. You and your men—"

"They ain't my men. We're the captain's men. Get that straight. He gives the orders."

"His orders will put you and that boy in there in your graves!"

He took her roughly by the arm and pulled her aside. "Ma'am, I've 'bout had my fill o' you an' your daughter. I don't wanna hear any more nonsense 'bout this, that or the other thing. Captain Lawson told me to wait here with the corporal, an' that's just what I aim to do."

"There are men coming, Mother," Tessa said from the window. "Looks to be Dr. Clemens, Mr. Gorman, and Mr. Hyde."

"Is the captain with them?" he asked.

Tessa didn't answer.

"I asked you a question, girl," he snapped. He went to the window and pushed her aside. When he saw the men approaching, he swore. Lawson wasn't with them. "Damn." Only two of the men were armed. If he was lucky, he might be able to take them both out before either one could get off a shot. He had to act now, though. He pulled back the hammer on his carbine.

"Which one's the doctor?" he asked Nan. "The old one?"

She nodded.

He went to open the door.

"No!" Tessa yelled, moving to intercept him. "Stop him, Mother!"

Nan tried to get hold of her, but the girl pushed her away and ran at Jordy. He put out a hand and stiff-armed her. She went sprawling.

"You pull somethin' like that again an' there'll be a bullet for you, missy. Now, sit still an' shut your damn mouth." Without waiting for her to reply, he threw open the door.

The sudden motion and sound of the door opening startled the men on horseback. The momentary hesitation was all Jordy needed. His first shot drove one of the men out of the saddle. He let the carbine fall and reached for his sidearm while the other two horsemen scattered. He fired and missed. Uttering a profanity, he took aim and fired again. The bullet struck the other rider in the chest and would have blown the man clean off his horse, but his boot got caught in the stirrup. The terrified horse bolted toward the wood, bouncing the dead man's head across the ground as it went. Jordy trained his weapon on the third rider, who now had his hands up in surrender.

"Don't shoot! Don't shoot! I'm the doctor!"

"Thought you might be." He waved the pistol at him. "Get down off that damn horse."

The doctor dismounted.

"Where's Captain Lawson?"

"In town, talking to Preacher John."

"Preacher who?"

"Preacher John."

Jordy kept the gun on him. "Corporal Boyd's inside. See to him."

The doctor removed his bag from where it was tied to the saddle and went into the house. Jordy followed him.

"Are you all right, Tessa?" the doctor asked when he caught sight of her sitting at the table, rubbing her head.

She pointed at Jordy. "He pushed me."

The doctor turned and shot him a contemptuous look. "You raised your hand to a girl, sir?"

Jordy lifted his foot and booted the man in the rear end. "I don't answer to any damn Reb, doctor or no. Now get your ass in that back room there an' see to my friend or it'll go hard with you."

Clemens picked himself up off the floor and went into the room where Boyd lay on the bed. Jordy watched from the doorway as the doctor pulled back the sheets and lifted the corporal's bloodstained shirt. When he turned to face Jordy again, the look in Clemens's eyes was grave.

"Can you help him?" Jordy asked.

He shook his head. "Surgery now would be useless. He's lost too much blood."

"More men coming, Sergeant!" Nan called out to him.

"Do what you can to make him comfortable," he said to the doctor. Then, he turned and went to the window. Another group of horsemen was coming up the hill. This time, he counted nearly twenty. He reloaded his weapons and then smashed the window with the barrel of his carbine.

One of the horsemen pulled away from the pack and drew rein a short distance from the porch.

"Sergeant! Come on out of there! We have your captain and you're vastly outnumbered!" The horseman called out. "There's no way out of this but to surrender!"

"Wrong, you Reb son of a bitch!"

Jordy pulled the trigger and watched as the upper right top quarter of the man's head disappeared. The horseman slumped over and fell from the saddle. Jordy started reloading, mumbling to himself about how much he hated Virginia as he pushed a cartridge into the Sharps carbine.

Two more men on horseback emerged from the pack. Jordy pushed the carbine's muzzle through the window, took aim, and touched his finger to the trigger. When he saw one of the men was Lawson, he loosened his hold on the weapon. The other horseman pointed a shotgun at the captain.

"Take another shot and he dies!"

Jordy pulled back from the window and kicked over a chair and the table. "Damn it, Goddamn it to Hell!"

"Come on out of there and throw your weapons down, Sergeant!" It was the horseman with the shotgun pointed at Lawson again. "Come on out of there now!"

Jordy went back to the window. "How do I know you ain't gonna shoot me, Reb?"

"You don't. But if you don't come out now, your captain dies."

Jordy looked at the others. Nan's eyes were downcast. He wasn't certain, but he thought he detected both fear and sorrow in her demeanor. Her daughter, though, held no such sentiments. On her face, he saw only malevolence and undisguised glee at his situation. As for the doctor, he simply nodded at the door and said, "They mean it, Sergeant. Fire another shot and you'll sign your captain's death warrant."

Jordy sighed and closed his eyes. After a few more moments, he swore under his breath again and opened the door. When he stepped outside, another horseman rode up and pointed his weapon at him. Jordy held his breath and waited to be shot.

"Your weapons. Throw them aside. Now."

He dropped the carbine and threw down his sidearm.

"Hands up, Sergeant."

Jordy pushed his hands into the air. His eyes went to Lawson, whose face remained expressionless.

Two horsemen rode up to him, dismounted, and bound his hands behind his back while a third strode up to the house and went inside. A moment later, he came back and yelled, "Their wounded man is in the back, just like the captain said."

The horseman pointing the gun at Lawson nodded. "Bring him on out of there, Multry. Tell the doctor to help you. Preacher John's got plans for him."

Jordy watched with a mixture of disbelief and rage when the man named Multry and Dr. Clemens emerged from the house with Boyd. They carried him out by his arms and legs. The boy shrieked in pain as they passed. When he heard it, Jordy exploded.

"What're you doin'? He's dyin', for Christ's sake! Just let 'im die in peace, God damn you! Just let 'im—"

One of the horsemen drove the butt of his shotgun into Jordy's stomach, doubling him over.

"Quiet, Yank."

It took a moment, but when Jordy got his breath, he spat in the man's face. "You goddamned traitor—"

The man grabbed a handful of Jordy's hair and wrenched his head to the side. "I told you to shut up."

"Fuck you, Reb."

The man smashed a fist into his face, knocking him over. He groaned and expelled a mouthful of dirt. Then, he was pulled back up to his feet. His attacker grinned at him.

"You ignorant trash, don't you know your friend there is one of the lucky ones? Maybe you and your captain will be, too."

"The hell're you jawin' 'bout, ya crazy Reb?"

"It's a real honor to be taken to the tree."

"The tree?"

"Old Hollow. It's where we all want to go in the end," the man said as if it was the most obvious thing in the world.

Jordy found the earnestness with which his captor spoke deeply unsettling. By nightfall, he would be more terrified than he had been since the first time he'd heard the infamous Rebel Yell at Bull Run.

Six

THE WHITE TREE

After Jordy's surrender at the Forrester house, the three Union soldiers were taken back into town. Boyd was placed under the care of Dr. Clemens, who had him taken to the apothecary, while Lawson and Jordy were placed in a holding cell at the constable's. A lone man armed with a shotgun closed the door and locked it.

Lawson turned to Jordy as soon as they were alone. "Are you hurt, Sergeant?"

"Broke my nose is all. Nothin' worth writin' home to my Aunt Edna 'bout. You?"

Lawson shook his head. "No. They had me covered before I could even get a shot off."

Jordy nodded. "I don't think these people are your ordinary run-of-the-mill Rebs."

"They're not." Lawson quickly recounted his conversation with the man called Preacher John and what he'd seen in the church. "There's something very definitely wrong in this place." He touched Jordy's shoulder. "It was a mistake coming here, Jordy. I should have listened to you. I'm sorry."

"You were just tryin' to help Boyd. I'd've done the same."

"No. You would have done what we were sent out here to do. Find Lee's army and report back to Sheridan."

Jordy shrugged. "Maybe. Maybe not. Don't hardly matter now. What we gotta do is find a way outta this godforsaken town."

"Agreed. But it won't be easy without horses and weapons."

"Whadda we do then, Captain?"

"We wait. Watch them. Look for a weakness, and when we find one, exploit it."

"What if one don't come our way for the takin'?"

"Then we do what you did back at the Forrester house," Lawson said. "What we'd do if we were in battle. Fight like hell and take as many of them with us as possible."

"I just hope I get the chance."

"Me, too." He sat down on a wooden bench that ran the entire length of the wall on the opposite side of the cell. "What was Corporal

Boyd's condition when you left him? I couldn't see him when we left the Forrester house."

"Bad. He's dyin'. Part of me hopes he passes before they do whatever they got planned for him. That son of a bitch who broke my nose said somethin' 'bout takin' Boyd to 'the tree.' Probably one like what you said you saw inna church." He balled his right hand into a fist and pounded it into his open palm. "I swear, I'm gonna get that Reb cocksucker—"

Lawson leaned over and patted his shoulder. "Save your strength, Sergeant. I don't know what's coming, but I have a feeling we're going to need every last ounce of it before this is done."

Jordy sighed and lay down on the opposite side of the bench. "I s'pose you're right."

They remained quiet for the next several hours. When dusk fell, the door opened and the guard came back in, this time accompanied by Peter, the man who had broken Jordy's nose, and Preacher John. The guard unlocked the cell door and, with Peter's help, bound Lawson's and Jordy's hands while the other man looked on. When they were done, they stepped aside to let Preacher John speak.

"Nightfall is upon us. It is time." He stood eye to eye with Lawson. "You and your man here needn't worry. It isn't *your* time. *Yet.*" He nodded at Peter and the guard, then turned and left.

The others took Lawson and Jordy by the arm and led them out of the cell and out into the open air. The guard fell in behind them with his shotgun cradled in his arms. Outside, a column of men, women, and children—all holding torches—stretched from the center of town up through the meadow and, as far as Lawson and Jordy could tell, well beyond the Forrester house. In the center of the road was a litter with a man at each corner.

"It's Boyd," Jordy whispered.

"I see him."

"He still alive?"

Just then, the four men each took a corner of the litter and lifted it from the ground, causing Boyd to cry out.

Lawson felt a pit form in his stomach. "It appears so." *Something tells me it would have been better if he'd died during the day, the Devil be damned.* He turned to Jordy and could tell by the look on the sergeant's face that he was thinking the same thing.

Preacher John stood in front of the litter and peered into the sky, then clasped his hands together as if he were about to offer up a prayer. What little chatter there had been disappeared, and the town square fell silent.

"The moon is full," he said. "Take him to the tree."

With that, he bowed his head, turned, and started to lead the four men carrying the litter down the road through the center of town. Peter turned and nodded at the two men standing guard over Lawson and Jordy.

"Bring them."

Lawson and Jordy felt the hard ends of shotgun barrels in their backs and started walking. They followed the same path as Preacher John and soon were close to the edge of town. When they reached the meadow, Lawson glanced over his shoulder and saw the townspeople had fallen in behind them. He estimated their number in the hundreds. As they came to the crest of the hill, the last rays of sunlight disappeared, casting the Forrester house in shadow. Standing on the porch were Nan and Tessa. When Preacher John came within a stone's throw of the house, the girl rushed toward him and threw herself at his feet.

"It's not fair, Preacher John, it's not fair!" Her face was streaked with tears. "It was my turn to go to the tree!" She grabbed hold of his britches. "My turn!"

His eyes held both gentleness and amusement. Touching her chin, he said, "Worry not, child. Your time shall come, I promise you. What I do this night, I do to give your mother time to steel herself against the inevitable." His gaze went to Nan. "I do it to show her I am not a hard-hearted man."

Tessa continued to cry. Preacher John glanced to his left, and two men broke from the procession to pull the girl away from him. Her eyes fell on Lawson and Jordy as she was carried back to her mother's porch.

"You!" she screamed, pointing at them. "You're the ones! You're why I can't go to the tree!" Her face was red with rage. "It was my turn! My turn, you righteous Yankee trash! My turn!"

The two men pushed the girl into her mother's arms. At first, she buried her head in Nan's chest, then suddenly lashed out with a series of screams and slaps, landing more than a few across her mother's face before being dragged inside.

The door slammed, muffling the sound of her cries, and Preacher John continued on toward the crest of the hill.

Behind the Forrester house, a thick forest came into sight. By now, the sky had gone black, and the land seemed afire from the orange glow of the torchlight. Eventually, Lawson and Jordy came to a well-trod footpath that led into the woods.

"We're almost there," Peter said, his voice animated with unmistakable excitement.

They pressed on into the forest. Not long after, the footpath gave way to a clearing, in the middle of which stood an immense tree. It was the same color as the moon—pale gray bordering on white —with a massive hole in the center that resembled some nightmarish creature's black, gaping maw. Its roots were like great gnarled feet, its branches a thousand jagged tentacles. Set off just a few feet from the tree was an upside-down cross. Its light brown wood was stained with what appeared to be dried blood and was scarred with deep scratches that might have been made by an animal's claws. When Lawson saw it, his eyes went to Preacher John. He met Lawson's gaze, then nodded at the four men, who proceeded to lift Boyd up from the litter and carry him, naked, toward the cross. Too weak to offer any resistance, the boy merely groaned in pain as the men used rope to secure his arms and legs.

Lawson stepped forward. "Preacher! Preacher John! Let him go! If you have to take someone, take me. Just let this boy die in peace. He deserves that much after what he's suffered."

Preacher John laughed. "You still don't understand, do you? Didn't my people tell you? This is a great honor. You saw the Forrester girl. How much she wants this. And you ask me to stop?"

"Not to stop. To take me instead." *It's no less than I deserve for bringing this insanity down on my men.*

Still smiling, Preacher John wagged a finger at Lawson. "I will tell you the same thing I told Tessa. Worry not. Your turn at the tree will come soon enough." He turned away and faced the tree, spreading out his arms like he was about to begin a sermon. "Come forth, O Dark Ones, and avail thee of our blood."

Within moments, a soft, low murmuring could be heard all around. The voices grew steadily louder until the forest was filled with a chorus of harsh, hissing whispers in a strange, indecipherable language. At first, Lawson was convinced the townspeople had begun some kind of sacrilegious chant, but then saw they were stone-faced and silent to a one. The voices grew louder. Some of the voices seemed to come from a distant part of the forest, while others sounded so close that he would have sworn someone was whispering in his ears. And though he did not recognize the words, their meaning was unmistakable. They were full of hate and contempt and mocking. And something else. Hunger. Ravenous hunger.

His eyes were drawn to the great tree. *Something's there. Something alive. Stirring. Awakening.* A black hand with inhumanly long fingers emerged from the tree's dark hollow and pressed its palm against the smooth, white bark. Then, another hand appeared, followed by thin, muscular forearms and shoulders, and, finally, a head.

"Jesus," Jordy said, breaking his silence. "Sweet Jesus Christ."

The creature crawled out from the hollow of the tree on all fours like one of those great cats from the swamps of Florida Lawson had read about before the war. It moved slowly, carefully, every movement calculated and full of purpose. When Boyd saw it, his eyes bulged in terror. Soon, another one followed, then another, until there was half a dozen. They were covered in tiny, black scales, with sharp, bony spikes protruding from their elbows. Their heads were crowned with long, thick, ram-like horns. They descended down the tree's massive trunk and surrounded Boyd, who began to scream.

"Don't let them hurt me, Captain! Please! Don't let them hurt me!"

Lawson fought a powerful urge to look away. "We're with you, Emil! We're right here!"

Boyd's eyes fell on Lawson and Jordy.

Lawson locked eyes with Boyd and nodded at him. "We're with you, Emil! We're with . . . " His voice trailed off.

One of the creatures pointed at the boy, then covered its mouth and let out a mean, guttural snicker. The others joined in, rasping at one another in their incomprehensible language until one of them—the first one out of the tree—opened its mouth and ran the tip of its tongue across Boyd's neck. Then, it licked the tips of its fingernails, drove its hand deep into the boy's chest, pulled out his heart, and devoured it.

That was too much for Jordy. His knees, which had begun to quake moments before, gave out from under him, and he fell to the ground, fighting to get in a breath as panic set in. Ignoring him and seeing that the feast was on, the creatures fell on Boyd like a pack of rabid animals. Within seconds, he was torn to pieces. Each of the creatures took a part of the boy in its mouth and retreated back near the tree. There, they proceeded to rend the muscle and sinew from bone with their jagged, catlike teeth, grunting and groaning as they filled their bellies. This went on for nearly an hour until bones licked clean of any sign of flesh began to fall to the ground where they formed a small pile before the upside-down cross. Finished, the creatures crawled down from the branches and back into the hollow, until only one—the one that had taken Boyd's heart—was left. It slinked down the tree toward the hollow, then stopped and fixed its eyes on Preacher John, who bowed his head in solemn response.

The creature's eyes passed over the townspeople once, then twice, before finally fixing on Lawson and Jordy. Then, it pointed one of its long, daggerlike fingers at them and let out a scream, a scream full of savage malice that pierced the night air and seemed to go on forever.

Lawson watched in disbelief as Jordy, his most reliable and unflappable scout, covered his ears and started to whimper. Finally, the scream came to an abrupt end, as if swallowed by the forest. Lawson looked away from Jordy in time to catch a glimpse of the creature's glowing red eyes before it vanished into the darkness of the great hollow.

Seven

DESPAIR

"I'm sorry, Captain, I don't know what came over me. I seen the elephant before, you know that, just never nothin' like what I saw last night."

Jordy's words sparked a fresh flash of memory of the previous night's horror in Lawson's mind. He shuddered and replied, "You've nothing to apologize for, Jordy. We've both seen the elephant. What happened to Emil ... Nothing can prepare a man for something like that."

"What were those things that come outta that tree?"

Lawson's voice was distant. "I don't know," he said, sighing. "The Dark Ones, they called them." He turned to Jordy. "Whatever they were, they are not of this world. That much I do know."

"And we're next on the menu, it 'pears."

Lawson nodded. "Yes, it appears so." Then, straightening up, he injected some energy into his voice and added, "We have time though, I think."

"Time for what?"

"To try and escape. If I heard Preacher John right, they only hold their ritual when the moon is full. That means we have about twenty-eight days before the end of the next lunar cycle."

Jordy stood and started to walk back and forth from one side of the cell to the other in an effort to stretch his legs. "That's all fine an' dandy, Captain, but what the hell do we do till then? Knock the next one who steps in here over the head?"

"No. They'll be expecting that. We need to find another way."

Jordy plopped himself back down on the bench. "Well, if you got any bright ideas, I'm game to hear 'em, cos I'm plumb out myself."

"Only one thing comes to mind at the moment."

"What's that?"

"Pray."

Jordy slumped a little bit where he sat. "Got to be honest with you, sir. Not sure what good prayin' will do. Don't seem to me like the good Lord is within hearin' distance of this place, if you know what I mean."

Lawson's eyes went to a window on the opposite side of the cell where early morning sunlight had just begun to creep inside. "Do you know the Book of Psalms, Jordy?"

"Nope. Never really been much of a churchgoin' man, to tell you the truth."

"Me neither. My mother was, though. She read the Bible every night before she went to bed. I remember during the winters in Pennsylvania she used to sit by the fire and hum to herself while she read from Psalms. There was one in particular she loved. Psalm 34. 'The Lord is nigh unto them who are brokenhearted; and saveth those who have no hope.' If you ask me, we've been without hope for going on five years now. Maybe, just maybe, we're due for our share of deliverance."

"That's a mighty nice sentiment, Captain, an' I don't disagree. But I'd still rather have my guns an' a crowd of those murderin' Reb bastards to shoot at."

Lawson nodded. "Me, too, Jordy. Me, too."

Eight

PRISONERS

A *week went by, then* two. During that time, Lawson and Jordy saw a regular rotation of guards—one stationed just outside the door, another stationed just inside. A different woman from town brought Lawson, Jordy, and the guards three meals per day. Once or twice a week, Dr. Clemens came by to make sure they weren't ill-used by their captors. He was, of course, always accompanied by a third guard armed with a shotgun.

"Preacher John wants you both in prime condition for when you go to the tree," Clemens informed them. "The Dark Ones, they prefer those that have some meat on their bones and a little vigor in the blood."

"They didn't seem none too particular 'bout tearin' Boyd apart," Jordy observed during one of the doctor's visits. "An' he was already half dead."

"Oh, well now, he was meaty enough for them, I suppose. Just didn't have much vigor left in him by the end."

The matter-of-factness with which Clemens delivered the statement almost made Jordy want to grab him by the neck and squeeze the life out of the old man, but Lawson had ordered him to keep his temper in check and not give Preacher John's people an excuse to punish them.

"Who are they, doctor?" Lawson asked. "The Dark Ones?"

"That's a spiritual matter and best left to the preacher to explain, which I'm sure he'll do in due time. I'm just here to make sure you're ready for when they take you to the tree."

"Any idea which one of us is goin' up there first?" Jordy asked.

"Preacher John makes that decision, and he hasn't yet seen fit to confide in me. But if I had my choice, it would be you, Sergeant Lightfoot. You have an ill-mannered way about you, one I find as repugnant as your accent. Peasant stock from Kentucky, is it?"

"It surely is."

Clemens pointed at him. "Aren't you wearing the wrong uniform? It's my understanding many of your brethren now wear Confederate gray."

"Well now, that's the difference between me an' them. They's a buncha traitors an' I ain't."

The doctor shrugged. "Either way, you'll soon be dead."

The burly cavalryman grinned at him. "Just so you know, doc, we get out o' here, first one I'm comin' after is you."

"Not the preacher?"

"No," he said. "The captain outranks me. Preacher John is his."

"I'll be sure to pass that along to him."

"See that you do," Jordy said.

The doctor shook his head, then nodded at the guard to let him pass out of the cell. "Typical arrogant Yankee trash," he muttered as he left.

When he was gone, Lawson turned to Jordy and said with a smile, "Now you've gone and upset the man."

"Well, whaddaya expect from a Kentucky peasant? Upsettin' Virginia snobs is what we do." He laughed as he said it. When he sat back down on the bench, however, his smile had been replaced by a scowl. "Still, I'd give real money for a chance to cut out his heart, Indian style. I read this book once 'bout the Plains Indians, an' the writer? He said that's what these Sioux warriors do to their enemies. Cut their hearts out with a dull blade."

"I'm surprised."

"That the Indians cut out peoples' hearts?"

"No. That you've actually read a book."

"Yep. Didn't even have no pictures or nothin' in it."

"Just words?"

"An' how. Never did get to finish it, though. Startin' to wonder if maybe I ever will."

"You will, Sergeant. You will."

Jordy didn't look convinced, though.

Nine

THE OFFER

DR. CLEMENS WAS RIGHT. WITHIN a few days, Preacher John had Lawson brought before him at the church. There, Lawson found him sitting alone in the front pew, just as he had the day he'd led his men into Old Hollow. The preacher had a thick, leather-bound volume in hand, which he closed and set down between them so Lawson could see the title engraved on the cover.

"*Evangelium Satanae.*" Lawson looked up at Preacher John. "The Gospel of Satan?"

"Just one of many names for this particular tome, Captain," Preacher John said, taking in a deep breath. "You must have many questions."

"I do. The Dark Ones—who and what are they?"

"They are creatures who were cast out of Heaven by the supposed One True God."

"Like in the poem by Milton?"

Preacher John swept his arms wide, as if he were about to begin a sermon. *"Better to reign in Hell, than serve in Heaven."* He smiled. "An educated man. I'm impressed. West Point?"

"Class of '54."

"I wasn't aware poetry was part of the curriculum at the academy."

"It was, but frankly, as much as I enjoyed reading it on the few occasions I could find the time to do so, I couldn't make heads or tails of it." He looked into the preacher's dark eyes. "But enough of that. Somehow, sir, I doubt you brought me here to discuss the likes of Milton."

"You are correct in your assumption."

"Then why?"

His eyes were piercing in their intensity. "I have need of men such as you, Captain. Men of will. Men of strength."

Lawson snorted, but said nothing.

"You sneer, but you know what I say is the truth. You do have courage. I have seen it. You offered yourself in his stead the night the Dark Ones took your man—"

"You mean, the night you murdered him."

Preacher John smiled. "Yes. I suppose you would think to see it that way."

"Is there any other way to see it?"

"I understand and respect your anger. Your rage. As I said, it's why I've asked you here."

"Asked me? I was brought here under guard. And you and your ... men ..." —he all but spat the last word out "—are holding me and Sergeant Lightfoot prisoner. Don't make it sound like you've extended a kind invitation to discuss scripture here in your ... *church* ... or whatever damnable name you have for this place."

"Captain, I feel as if our conversation has taken a turn. Gone astray, so to speak. I have no wish to continue verbally sparring with you. We are short on time. In just a few days, the moon will be full again, and I will have to choose which one of you will be taken to the tree. I would rather it not be you. That is to say, I *hope* it will not be you." He paused before continuing. "Your Northern armies have won the war, Captain Lawson. Soon, the South will fall. We both know that. Now, by and large, my people keep to themselves and have done so for generations. Yes, on occasion, we have been forced to fight off Yankee raids since the war began or get involved like Major Forrester did, to keep up appearances, as they say. That is why I need men like you after the guns go silent and the peace is made. Soon, every county in Virginia will be overrun with Yankees. Yankees with one thing and one thing only on their minds. Making money by exploiting little towns that were happy to keep to themselves. Towns like Old Hollow."

"You want me ... to join you."

"Yes, I do. I think you would be a most prized asset to us here in Old Hollow. You are an intelligent and resourceful man, that much is evident, and you know the ways of the North. My offer also has the added benefit, of course, of being predicated on your life being spared."

"What happens to Jordy? He's a man of strength. A man of character, as you say."

Preacher John wrinkled his nose. "I think not, sir. I think you and I both know that there is no taming that one. His is a wild and violent nature, and not predisposed, I think, to acclimating to life here in Old Hollow."

"And you think me different?"

"You have the advantage, in my judgment, of being a highly adaptable creature, Captain." He placed his hand on the book between them. "Come with me. I can teach you everything you need to take your place at my side. You haven't even the slightest inkling yet as to the fruits of life you could enjoy here in Old Hollow, if you would only stand up with me. You have seen our town. It is not like other towns in Virginia. It is largely untouched by the war, is it not? Do our men and women look like they are starving? Do our children go naked in the cold? No. Because we are protected. Protected by the Dark Ones. They provide us with everything we need. And all they ask in return is a little bit of our blood, which is freely given. *Happily* given." Another pause. "Or, you can go to the tree. I must say, I truly believe you to be one of the luckiest, no

... one of the most blessed men I have ever met."

"In what way?"

"Few men, Captain, are fortunate enough to have their destiny so clearly laid out before them. All you have to do, my friend, is choose. Life here in Old Hollow, or death at the tree."

Lawson shook his head and stood. "Preacher, I think I'd prove to be more trouble than I'm worth to a man like you. You'd do just as well to kill me now and save yourself a whole lot of grief. Keeping me around here any longer than necessary would prove to be a terrible mistake."

Preacher John's brows went up. "Very well. It's the tree for you then." He nodded at the men who had escorted Lawson from the jail. "Take Captain Lawson back to his cell."

Ten

THE DARK ONES

Lawson found it more and more difficult to sleep as the next full moon approached. The nights were the hardest, and he was haunted by a recurring nightmare. In the dream, he rode up a long and wide country lane to a small farmhouse where a woman he had never met before but somehow knew to be Emil Boyd's mother stood waiting for him. Tears had already formed in her eyes by the time he dismounted and walked up the steps to deliver the news of her son's death. He caught her as she crumpled to the floor and started to sob, and tried to tell her that Emil had died bravely fighting the Rebels on the field of battle.

"Liar!" she screamed, her eyes full of hate. She raked her nails across his cheek, drawing blood. "You *let* him die! Just like all the others! You led my boy to his death like a lamb to the slaughter!"

He tried to pull away, but her grip was inhumanly strong. She raised her hand for another strike, only this time, her hand was black, and her nails long, sharp claws. He cried out as she drove her hand into his chest and then woke up, drenched in sweat.

"'Nother dream, Captain?" Jordy asked.

Lawson nodded.

"Same one as before?"

"Yes."

"Bad dreams is part of soldierin', I suspect."

"I suspect you're right."

"Bet they don't tell you that at West Point."

He nodded. "The instructors failed to mention it."

Jordy patted him on the shoulder. "I know it ain't proper for me to be talkin' to you this way, you bein' an officer an' all an' me an enlisted, but you got to let up on yourself some, Captain. Soldiers go to war. Some of 'em don't come back. That's the truth, an' there ain't no denyin' it. An' you beatin' yourself up over it ain't gonna bring 'em back an' it sure as shit ain't gonna help us none now. I know you think you done wrong bringin' us here instead o' goin' back to Sheridan, but you ask me, I'd rather serve under an officer who puts his men first than some damn martinet bent on blazin' a path to glory without much account for the cost. Maybe you do care too much, sir, but if that's the worst thing you got to answer for when you step in front o' the Creator, you'll probably do okay."

Lawson met his eyes. "Thank you, Jordy."

"What I said, it probably don't make it any easier, I guess."

"Not really. But as you're so fond of saying, I appreciate the sentiment."

Jordy was about to reply when the door opened, and Nan Forrester walked in with a large basket in hand.

"Hello, Nan," the guard greeted her.

"Horace, hello," she said pleasantly.

"Guess it's your turn to bring these two their dinner, eh?"

"And yours as well." She placed the basket on the table and opened it. "Hot soup for you, Horace, I hope you like it."

Horace sniffed at the steaming bowl of soup. "Smells good. What kind is it?"

"Artichoke soup. And for our friends," she said as she turned toward the cell, "a little roast pig, some bread, and a pound cake."

Horace frowned. "They get all that?"

"Preacher John wants them strong. You know the way of things around here, Horace."

"Yes, I suppose I do." He glanced at the soup. "May I?"

She nodded. "Of course. I'll wait for you to finish and then perhaps you could open the cell so I can feed these men."

He nodded and began to spoon the artichoke soup into his mouth, spilling more than a few drops in his dark beard along the way. While the guard ate, Nan walked over to the cell where she folded her hands at her waist and looked directly into Lawson's eyes.

"How's Tessa?" Horace asked. "Still fussing over getting bumped back a few notches by these two Yanks?"

"Yes. Still upset." Her eyes remained fixed on Lawson.

"Well, can't say as I blame her. These young ones. Always crazy to get their turn at the tree." He held the bowl up to his mouth and swallowed the last of the soup. "You've done a good job raising her, Nan, especially with Robert being gone now. She probably just wants to do her part for Old Hollow."

Nan nodded. "For Old Hollow, yes." Her voice was devoid of almost any feeling. "All we do is for Old Hollow."

He pushed the soup bowl aside. "Well, thanks for that, Nan. It was a real treat."

"I'm so glad you found it so."

"Well, I suppose I ought to let you feed these two now," he said as he got out of the chair.

He'd gone no more than a step or two toward the cell when he hesitated and started to stumble.

"Are you all right, Horace?" she asked.

He pressed a hand to his forehead and blinked several times. "Feel a little woozy, actually."

His next attempt at taking a step resulted in his tripping over his own feet. He started to fall to the floor, but Nan caught him.

"Horace?" she said. "Let me help you."

She put his arm over her shoulder and led him back to the chair.

"Don't ... don't feel so ... so ... good ..." His voice slurred as he spoke.

"You just rest now," she said, patting his back. "Rest now."

A moment later, he was unconscious. Nan took the keys from a ring on the wall and walked over to the cell. Lawson and Jordy watched in disbelief as she slipped the key into the lock.

"Before I let you out of there," she said to Lawson, "I want your solemn promise as a Union officer that you'll get me and my daughter out of here."

Lawson and Jordy exchanged looks of shock. After a moment, Lawson said, "I suspect, Sergeant, that we aren't going to get a better opportunity than this."

"My sentiments exactly, sir."

Lawson met her gaze. "You have my word. We'll do everything we can."

"All right then, gentlemen." She unlocked the cell. "Come out of there."

Free of the cell, he asked her, "Our weapons?"

"Close by."

"What 'bout our horses?" Jordy asked. "We ain't gonna get very far without 'em."

"Also close by."

Lawson touched Nan's arm. "Why are you doing this, Mrs. Forrester?"

She frowned. "Are you a father, Captain?"

"Yes, I am. I have a daughter. She'd be about seven now."

"Then you shouldn't have to ask why I'm doing this. Not all of us are eager to see our children sacrificed in the name of the devilry that's taken hold of this town."

He nodded. "Understood."

She pointed at the pan containing the pound cake. "There's a knife buried in the middle of that. You'll need it for the guard outside."

Jordy dug his fingers into the yellow cake and pulled out the knife. "Got it." He took a few bites of the cake while he examined the knife. "Where'd you get this?"

"It was my husband's. It's one of the few possessions of his the First Virginia saw fit to return to me."

Jordy's eyes grew somber. "Wonder how many Yankee troops he stuck with this thing."

She started to retort, but Lawson cut her off.

"Now is not the time, Sergeant," he said. "We have to go."

Jordy nodded. "I'll handle the guard."

"Mrs. Forrester, if you would create a distraction of some kind, we should be able to overtake him easily." He motioned for Jordy to follow him in positioning himself behind the door, then nodded at Nan.

She opened the door. "Matthew? Something's wrong with Horace. I think you ought to come have a look."

The guard's voice carried inside. "Is he sick?"

"I ... I'm not sure."

"Maybe I ought to get Dr. Clemens."

"No, please, just have a look first, if you would be so kind."

A moment passed, and then the guard came inside. Nan closed the door and stepped back as Jordy and Lawson pounced. The guard never even had time to shout. Jordy pressed the blade to his neck and pulled, opening the man's throat. He fell to the floor, gagging on his own blood, and was dead within minutes. Lawson took up the man's shotgun and searched through his pockets where he found two extra cartridges.

"Are there any more of them outside?" he asked her.

"No, they're all at the church. Preacher John always gives a special sermon the night they take someone to the tree." She opened the door. "Follow me."

The cool night air felt good on their faces after spending weeks inside the musty confines of the holding cell. Lawson looked up at the sky, saw the moon was full, and nudged Jordy.

He snorted. "No sense doin' today what you could put off till tomorrow, eh, Mrs. Forrester?"

She turned on him. "Sergeant, if I could have gotten to you and your captain sooner, I would have. This was the first opportunity I had to get to you two men while most of the town was distracted. Of course, if the conditions of your rescue aren't to your liking, you could always get back in your cell."

Jordy smiled. "I'm startin' to like you, ma'am, even if you are a class-A Virginia snob."

She shook her head, exasperated, then led them around the back of the constable's office and through a thick grove of trees. Lawson smelled the stables long before he was able to make them out in the dark. A thin smile formed on his lips at the familiar fragrance of horse manure, oats, and hay. A few moments later, they reached the stables. The horses had already been saddled.

When Jordy saw their weapons on a table near the horses, he turned to Nan and tipped the brow of his hat to her. "Virginia snob or no, I'm obliged to you, ma'am."

She ignored him.

Lawson mounted and watched as Nan pulled herself up onto her own horse.

"Where's your daughter?" he asked, confused.

"Up at the house, asleep. She would not come willingly, so I had to give her the same draught I gave to Horace."

"Wonderful," Jordy said. "Captain, we got to hightail it out of here."

"I gave my word, Jordy. That has to stand for something."

"I knew you'd say somethin' like that," he grumbled. "Least we got these." He held up his Dragoon pistol and carbine for Lawson to see.

"Indeed." Lawson replied, loading his pistol. He gestured at his saber as he attached it to his belt. "I'm grateful for this. It belonged to my father."

"If it's all the same to you, Captain, I agree with Sergeant Lightfoot. Time is of the essence. Escape first, thank you's later."

"Of course." He turned to Jordy. "We'll need to keep the horses at a walk for now. It's our best chance at remaining undetected."

"There's a game trail through the woods to the east we can take that leads up near the house. It would keep us off the main road," Nan said.

"Good."

They walked the horses out of the stable and soon entered a forested area. There, they came upon the trail. It took less than ten minutes at a slow walk to reach the house.

"Jordy, help Mrs. Forrester with her daughter and then let's be rid of this place."

"Yes, sir."

The sergeant dismounted and followed Nan inside. While he waited, Lawson did his best to keep the horses quiet and watch for intruders. The former was not hard. Most Union cavalry scouts chose mounts that demonstrated the ability to remain calm under fire, a trait even more critical to scouting work where stealth was often the difference between discovery by the enemy and keeping one's presence concealed. Aside from a soft nicker here and there, the horses remained quiet.

Just a few minutes later, Nan and Jordy emerged from the house, the latter with Tessa's bundled-up form in his arms. She let out a soft moan as he put her in the saddle. A moment later, he climbed atop the horse and took the reins.

"Ready, Captain."

Lawson looked backward at Nan. "Can we take the same way out of town?"

"The game trail doesn't go as far as the edge of Old Hollow, but it will get us close."

"Very well."

He tapped the spurs against the horse's flanks and they reentered the forest. The four of them moved slowly back down the game trail, close enough to town to see the bright glow of kerosene lamps through the church's windows and hear the shouts and cries of people responding to what Lawson guessed was another one of Preacher John's sermons.

"How long until the guard is relieved?" Lawson asked Nan. "The one who was standing outside."

"I'm sorry, I don't know. It could be a matter of minutes or a matter of hours."

"Better move with a purpose when we get out of shoutin' distance of this place then," Jordy said.

Lawson nodded. "Agreed."

The last of the lights dwindled away just as the game trail came to an end and they found themselves close to the stables and the apothecary.

Lawson looked up at the moon, whose pale light illuminated the main road leading out of Old Hollow. He took a deep breath and tried to keep his mount hidden within the thin sliver of shadow that skirted the edge of the road. They hadn't gone far when Tessa began to moan.

"Quiet, girl," Jordy whispered, clamping a hand over her mouth.

That only seemed to make her struggle more. Though still half asleep, she frowned and called out to Nan. "Mother?"

Lawson drew rein. "Calm your daughter. We won't get very far if she cries out."

Jordy pulled up next to Lawson's mount. Nan leaned over and gently ran the tips of her fingers over the girl's cheek.

"I'm here, Tessa. I'm here. Go back to sleep. All is well." She brushed a stray hair out of Tessa's eyes and repeated, "All is well."

That appeared to quiet the girl, and they were once more underway. The road out of Old Hollow remained narrow and rocky, forcing them to move slower than Lawson would have preferred. Soon, however, they left the town behind. When a thick bank of clouds rolled in and swallowed up the moonlight, he was grateful for the sudden, unexpected cover the darkness provided.

"Maybe our luck'll hold up, Captain," Jordy said, obviously feeling the same way.

"Maybe."

After a few miles, the road widened into a turnpike, and they increased speed to a full gallop. They maintained that pace for more than five miles before the horses began to tire. Lawson signaled to pull up.

"Let them get their second wind while we find out where we are," he said, rummaging through the saddlebag until he found the map. Turning to Nan, he said, "I see you thought of everything."

"I'm not one to leave much to chance, Captain," she replied.

"Nor am I," he said, spreading the map out. "Any idea where we are?"

She studied the map for a moment, then pointed. "There. About ten miles from Cumberland."

Lawson rolled up the map and stuffed it back into the saddlebag. "All right. Maybe someone there will know where either army is."

"Hell, Captain, for all we know, the war could be over."

"You really believe we could be that lucky?"

Jordy spat. "Prob'ly not."

"Mother?"

The sound of Tessa's voice interrupted the two men. They turned to find Nan's daughter fully awake.

"Where am I?" she asked, her eyes falling on Jordy. Recognition registered in her eyes almost immediately. She tried to pull away from him and get off the horse. "No! Let go! Mother! Where are we? What are we doing out here in the middle of the night!?"

"Quiet, Tessa!" Nan ordered her. "These men are taking us away from Old Hollow for good."

That enraged her daughter. She slapped at Jordy and yelled, "No! I want to go back! It was my turn! It was my turn! I want to go back!"

Nan reached over and grabbed her sleeve. "Enough, Tessa! We are *never* going back. Never."

"I hate you!" the girl screamed at her mother. "You're jealous, that's all! Jealous because the Dark Ones wanted me! *Me!*"

Nan slapped the girl, abruptly bringing her cries to an end. Tessa recoiled, her hands frozen in place in front of her face.

"Not another word, Tessa," she warned. "Not another word."

Lawson pulled Nan back. "We should go. There are still several hours before morning. If we keep moving, we can make Cumberland by first light." He turned his attention to Tessa. "Miss Forrester, if I have to, I will have Sergeant Lightfoot bind and gag you the rest of the way. I don't want to, but I will if you put me in a position where I have to. Is that clear?"

She refused to answer.

"Tessa, answer Captain Lawson now or, by God, I'll slap you till your face is black and blue," her mother threatened.

"Yes, it's clear. *Damn Yankee trash.*"

Lawson held up a hand when he saw a look in Jordy's eyes that made it clear the sergeant was at the end of his patience with the young woman. "Good. Then we should be on ... our ... way ..." His voice trailed off as he glanced past Jordy's mount and searched through the darkness.

"Captain?" Nan asked. "What is it? Do you hear—"

"Quiet."

Within moments, they all heard it. The sound of approaching horses.

"Goddamn it," Jordy swore, then hushed long enough to listen more closely to the sound of hoofbeats getting closer. "At least ten horses, Captain. More than that maybe."

Lawson's heart began to pound, a reaction to approaching danger to which he had grown accustomed over the last five years. He began to study their surroundings, looking for some tactical advantage.

"We can't outrun 'em with the ladies, an' we can't fight 'em if there's as many as I think there are," Jordy said.

"Not mounted we can't," Lawson said.

Jordy's brows furrowed into a frown. "What're you on 'bout, Captain?"

"If we can find some cover, we might have a chance," he replied, his eyes finally landing on a pile of fallen trees about twenty feet up the side of the turnpike. He pointed at them. "There. That might work."

Jordy nodded. "Fight dismounted? Good idea, Captain."

Lawson spurred his horse and took off up the road. Jordy fell in right behind him. A few moments later, they had dismounted and wrapped the horses' reins around a nearby tree. The men loaded their weapons. When they were done, Lawson took a thick, dirty handkerchief and a length of rope from his saddlebag and turned to Nan and Tessa.

"I don't trust her," he said, pointing at the daughter. "And I can't have her running off or giving our position away. She'll have to be bound and gagged until this is over."

"No!" Tessa screamed. "No!"

Jordy stood and pushed his Dragoon revolver into her face. "Shut up."

She fell quiet.

"Is this necessary, Captain?" Nan asked.

"Completely."

"Horsemen comin'," Jordy said.

Lawson turned the girl around and tied her hands, then gagged her mouth with the handkerchief. As soon as she was quiet and secured, he took up a position behind one of the fallen tree trunks next to Jordy. The sound of the approaching horsemen grew louder.

"Close now, Captain," Jordy said.

Lawson nodded and took up his carbine. "Wait for the first few to pass," he said. "You take the lead riders. I'll concentrate fire on the stragglers."

"Yes, sir."

The first three riders came into view and rode past. Jordy took down the first man with a shot from his carbine, which he quickly put aside in favor of his pistol. A moment later, more riders came into view. Lawson counted six and unloaded his first shot at the rider bringing up the rear. The man fell from the saddle, and his horse ran off. Jordy continued to fire his Dragoon pistol while Lawson took up the shotgun he'd taken from the guard back in Old Hollow. Two more of the riders fell before the rest of them began to return fire. None of their pursuers' shots found a target, though. It was too dark for them to see well enough, and most of their mounts were not accustomed to the sound of gunfire, which made them impossible to control. Lawson and Jordy, on the other hand, had the advantages of long years of training and a well-chosen position that was both fixed and provided ample cover. Within minutes, there were only three riders left alive, hidden behind the fallen bodies of their wounded horses.

Jordy reloaded while Lawson provided enough covering fire to pin the remaining riders down. Then, Jordy did the same for him. The exchange of fire became more intermittent.

"You men ought to surrender!" Lawson yelled in between shots fired. "Throw your weapons down and we'll let you ride out of here alive!"

A few moments later, a familiar voice rang out in the dark.

"Captain Lawson!"

"I hear you, Preacher John. Go ahead."

"You are still outnumbered three to two. And there are more on the way."

"Let 'em come!" Jordy yelled back. "I could shoot at you Rebs all night!"

"I wasn't talking about Rebels, Sergeant."

Lawson and Jordy exchanged a look of dread. They both knew what the preacher would say next.

"They're on their way now, even as we speak," Preacher John said.

"And they hunger. Oh, how they hunger."

Lawson pointed at the horses. "We have to get out of here. Now."

"No argument there, sir," Jordy replied. "Problem is, we try to take off, those gunmen there got the drop on us. They'd pick us off before we got very far."

"The forest isn't an option, either. It'd be slow going, and those creatures would be on us before we could escape, if what he says is true." Lawson held out his hand. "Give me your weapons."

"Huh?"

"I said give me your weapons. I'll hold off the preacher and his men while you and the women escape up the turnpike. You'll have to go hard to put some distance between us, so don't let them slow down."

Jordy shook his head. "Captain, I ain't doin' that."

He grabbed the sergeant's carbine out of his hands. "You'll do it and you'll do it now."

"I ain't leavin' you here."

"Jordy, give me your pistol. That's an order."

"No." Jordy said, shaking his head emphatically. "I ain't doin' it."

"I said *give* it to me." He yanked the pistol out of Jordy's hand. "Your cartridges, too. I'll need all the ammunition I can lay hands on."

"Sir, please—"

"Every second you sit there blubbering at me instead of doing as you're ordered to do allows those creatures to get closer." He pointed at

Nan and Tessa. "Are you really going to condemn them to the kind of death that awaits them if you stay?"

Jordy slumped a little. "I don't care 'bout them. They're goddamned Reb traitors."

"That may be true, but I gave Mrs. Forrester my word. Would you make a liar out of me, Sergeant?"

Jordy grew quiet. Then, he handed over the box of cartridges for his carbine and the pistol. "The hell'm I s'posed to tell Sheridan?"

"Anything other than the truth. Do that and you're liable to be court-martialed and locked up in an asylum."

Jordy nodded, unable to look his commanding officer in the eye. "Good-bye, Captain."

"Good-bye. And Jordy?"

"Yes, sir?"

"If you do make it back, keep your head down. Something tells me Bob Lee's boys don't have much fight left in them. Maybe if you're lucky, you'll get to see Alvena and those little ones of yours again soon."

Jordy turned and crawled toward Nan and Tessa. "Get her ready. We're leavin'."

"But what about Captain—"

"Just move, ma'am. Before I change my mind." He turned to Lawson and nodded. "Go ahead, sir. I'm ready."

Lawson peered into the darkness again, looking for shadows and movement. A moment later, he heard the sound of a horse grunting from behind him. Jordy had the women mounted and had climbed into the saddle. Keeping one hand on the other horse's reins, he applied the spurs to his own. The animal's loud whinny alerted the gunmen from Old Hollow that something was afoot. Two of them peeked their heads above their now-dead horses and took aim. Lawson fired, and one of them fell. The other, distracted, concentrated his fire on Lawson's position, but missed. That was enough time for Jordy. He broke through the edge of the forest and out onto the turnpike, the other horse in tow. Lawson fired his pistol and watched the other man fall. By the time the smoke from the gunfire cleared, the hoofbeats from the fleeing horses already sounded far away.

He reloaded his carbine, holstered his pistol, and glanced up into the night sky. The moon was full.

"I suppose it's just you and me now, Preacher John."

"Not for long. They're close. I can *feel* them."

Lawson's eyes scanned the darkness, looking for movement. There was nothing but the forest and a road full of dead men and horses. "I don't suppose you intend to surrender, do you?"

"No self-respecting Southerner would ever surrender to the likes of you."

"Then you leave me no choice but to come and get you myself."

"Come forward then, and try, Captain."

Lawson closed his eyes and tried to picture his wife and daughter the last time he had seen them, waving to him from the porch of their home in Pennsylvania as he'd ridden away, back to the war. It had been in October 1862, just after Antietam. His daughter, Ada, blew him kisses, her eyes twinkling in the morning sunlight while his wife did her best not to cry, for fear of upsetting the little one. He smiled, opened his eyes, and stood.

Preacher John opened fire with a revolver. The first shot missed Lawson by a wide margin. The second grazed his arm. Lawson winced and tucked the stock of the carbine snug into his shoulder. The preacher fired again. The cartridge slammed into Lawson's stomach and almost doubled him over, but he somehow managed to keep his feet. He took aim and fired. Preacher John cried out and clutched his right shoulder, losing his weapon in the process. The carbine spent, Lawson drew his Dragoon pistol and leapt over the horse carcass, pinning Preacher John to the ground with his knees. He pressed the barrel to the preacher's forehead.

"You should have killed me at the tree when I offered myself in that boy's place."

"Yes, I suppose I should have. It hardly matters now, though. Soon, they'll be upon us, and you'll be dead. Torn to pieces, like your dear Corporal Boyd."

Lawson pulled back the hammer on the Dragoon pistol. "I'm not afraid to die."

"No, I suppose you're not." Preacher John laughed, then immediately started to cough in pain. Blood appeared at the corner of his mouth. "Are you going to kill me now?"

Lawson eased his knees up from the preacher's shoulders and stood, his pistol still trained on the man's head. "No. I think I'll let them do it." He fired a shot into the preacher's right leg, then put one in his left leg. "Just to make sure you don't get any fancy ideas about running away."

The man writhed in pain, his eyes seething with hatred.

"What's wrong, Preacher?" Lawson asked, grunting from the pain of his stomach wound. "Sacrifice to the Dark Ones is what everyone in Old Hollow was born for. Isn't that what you told me? Or does that only apply to wounded men who can't defend themselves? Or children who know no better?"

Preacher John reached for the revolver on the ground, but Lawson was too quick for him. He kicked the weapon away.

"No, I don't think so," he told him. "Your fate will be the same as the countless men, women and children you've murdered in the name of whatever unholy beasts you worship in that town of yours."

The preacher started to retort, then froze. His eyes were fixed on something behind Lawson, who turned to find two shadowy figures with glowing red eyes in the middle of the turnpike. They lay prone on the ground, ready to pounce.

"Good-bye, Preacher," he said, turning to face the shapes in the road.

Harsh rasps and whispers filled the night air, but Lawson ignored them. He started walking toward the creatures and lined up a shot. As he moved, a passage from a poem with which he'd become acquainted during his final year at West Point flashed through his mind. It had been a new poem at the time, appearing in all the popular magazines. The academy's English composition instructor had forced the cadets in his charge to commit the entire poem to memory, though Lawson was damned if he could remember the title or author. One particular stanza came back to him as he fired:

> "Storm'd at with shot and shell,
> Boldly they rode and well,
> Into the jaws of Death,
> Into the mouth of Hell"

The shadows in the road scattered at the sound of the shot, and then they were on him, biting and pulling and tearing. He had time to let out a single piercing wail before a pair of hands clamped down on both of his temples, and all went black as the night.

Acknowledgements

It's often said that writing a book is a solitary endeavor, and, to some degree, that's true. However, *publishing* a book is an entirely different story, and *Old Hollow* would never have seen the light of day if it weren't for the work and support of a number of people. So, I'd like to express my gratitude to the following individuals for all their time and effort:

Olivia Raymond, owner of **Aurelia Leo**, for taking the time to read the story and for seeing its potential when so many other editors and publishers responded to me with a "Thanks, but no thanks, kid. Better luck next time."

Old Hollow's primary editor, **Luann Reed-Siegel**, whose sharp eye and attention to detail kept me honest and made the book (and this writer) better.

The book's cartographer and illustrator, **Tiphaine Leard**, who helped bring the town of Old Hollow to life with some amazing renderings.

Thomas Deckard Croix, for the compelling and vivid voice work he delivered on the audiobook version of *Old Hollow*.

My good friends, **Tracy Olsen and Owen Linderholm**, both of whom took time out of their busy schedules to read early drafts of *Old Hollow*. Their initial feedback was indispensable in terms of helping me polish the story before I ever submitted it for publication.

My parents, **Lydia and David**, who recognized early on that I might have a future as a writer and encouraged me every step of the way from the time I was nine years old.

And, of course, my wife, **Tanya**, who, as the first reader on every single story I've written over the past seven years, has provided invaluable encouragement and support at those critical times when her husband was close to throwing up his hands and packing it in because the words stubbornly refused to come.

Thank you, all.

A.S.

About the Author

Ambrose Stolliker lives in the Pacific Northwest with his wife and son. His stories have been published in *Ghostlight Magazine, Sex and Murder Magazine, Hungur Magazine, Sanitarium Magazine, Stupefying Stories,* Tincture Journal and the *State of Horror: Louisiana Volume II* anthology from Charon Coin Press. He is a former newspaper reporter and magazine journalist and is currently a storyteller and social media manager in the technology sector.

For more information, please visit:

www.ambrosestolliker.wordpress.com

Made in the USA
Middletown, DE
03 August 2021